TIME WARP TRIO

Time Warp Trio™ is produced by WGBH in association with Soup2Nuts for Discovery Kids.

Harper Trophy® is a registered trademark of HarperCollins Publishers.

Time Warp Trio®: Wushu Were Here
Copyright © 2007 WGBH Educational Foundation and Chucklebait, Inc.
Artwork, Designs and Animation © 2006 WGBH Educational Foundation.
All rights reserved. Printed in the United States of America.
No part of this book may be used or reproduced in any manner whatsoever without written permission except in the case of brief quotations embodied in critical articles and reviews. For information address HarperCollins Children's Books, a division of HarperCollins Publishers, 1350 Avenue of the Americas, New York, NY 10019.
www.harpercollinschildrens.com

Library of Congress catalog card number: 2006929491
ISBN-13: 978-0-06-111645-2 — ISBN-10: 0-06-111645-9

Book design by Joe Merkel
❖
First Harper Trophy edition, 2007

Time Warp Trio

Wushu Were Here

Time Warp Trio created by
Jon Scieszka
Adapted by
Jennifer Frantz
Adapted from the teleplay by
Raye Lankford

HarperTrophy®
An Imprint of HarperCollinsPublishers

CHAPTER 1

"So you are afraid to fight? Perhaps you fear that you are not strong enough?" a voice said.

Anna, Fred, and I peeked out from the skinny bamboo trees we were hiding behind. In a small clearing we saw two angry-looking guys dressed in ancient-looking Chinese robes. They were both holding wooden fighting staffs and looked ready to rumble.

"Not strong enough?" the second guy replied. "I'll show you strength. *HEEYAAH!*"

He swung his fighting staff at angry guy number one. The end of the staff smacked into the ground with a thud. Angry guy number one had vanished into thin air.

Suddenly he reappeared right beside angry guy number two.

"*AAAAAAAAAAAHHHHH!*" Angry Two screamed as if he'd seen a ghost. He dropped his staff and fled in shock.

"Go to your village!" Angry One yelled. "Send me your best fighters and I will test their strength."

Then he picked up the other staff on the ground. He looked a little disappointed that the fight hadn't lasted longer.

"Is there no one in China who is up to the task?" he said to no one in particular. He tossed Angry Two's staff into the air, sending it flying in Fred's direction.

"Ow! Hey!" Fred yelled. "It's raining weapons." He picked up the staff that had just smacked him on the head. "Hey, Joe," he said, showing it to me. "Look at this cool fighting staff!"

Fred swung the staff wildly and struck his best kung fu pose.

"Maybe you should put that down," Anna suggested.

I gave Anna a look. It was her fault we were in this mess—stuck in the middle of a forest in ancient China with Fred waving a weapon and an angry Chinese warrior guy five feet away.

"This is all because you went digging in my things," I said.

"Well, I wouldn't have dug," Anna said, "if you'd just told me what wushu is."

"Silence!" a voice screamed.

Angry One had spotted us. "You," he said, looking at Fred. "You will go first."

Fred looked at his staff and then back at the angry guy who was now in a fighting stance. "Something tells me we're not playing stickball," Fred said.

Angry One pulled his knee into his chest and then slid in Fred's direction. Fred ducked. Anna and I dived back toward our bamboo hiding place.

Fred tried to stand up, but suddenly Angry One was an inch from his face.

"Wha . . . ?" Fred cried.

"You are fast, my friend," Angry One said. "But not fast enough."

"*KYAAAAAAH!*" He whipped his staff at Fred, who fell to the ground.

Anna and I ran to Fred. "Are you okay?" I asked.

No reply. Fred wasn't moving.

"Wake up!" Anna cried.

Angry One looked down at us with an evil stare. "I have finished off your friend," he said. "Who is next?"

CHAPTER 2

Poor Fred. He never saw it coming. I blame it all on that kung fu movie. . . .

We were back in Brooklyn hanging out in my room, watching a movie about these two guys from seventh-century China, Li Shimin and Wang.

"I knew you were behind this, Wang."

"Where are your monks when you need them, Li Shimin?"

See, Li Shimin was the good guy who'd been kidnapped by Wang, the bad guy. Now Li Shimin's thirteen monk friends were going to take on Wang's entire army to get their pal back. But at the moment, Li Shimin and Wang were going to duke it out man-to-man.

They both raised their fighting staffs.

"Awesome!" Fred said. "Time for an old-fashioned booty-whoopin', kung fu–style."

Li Shimin and Wang slid carefully around each other like two cobras waiting to strike. Suddenly . . . *whap, whap*. The staffs slammed into each other. They battled back and forth for a few minutes. Then Wang landed a real whammy. Li Shimin was about to crumple. Then . . .

"Do you suffer from uncontrollable drooling? Well, now there's help."

"Oh, man," I said.

"There's always a commercial just at the exciting part."

"Is the good guy really dead?" Anna asked.

"Nah," Fred said. "He's the hero. They'd never kill the hero in the first five minutes."

Fred jumped up into his own kung fu stance. "That guy playing Li Shimin is so cool," he said. "He's got great wushu." Fred did a wild kick, knocking over the lamp on my desk.

"'Wushu?' What's that?" Anna asked.

Fred ignored Anna and chopped at the air. "I'd love to try out some wushu on my older brother, Mike. *WAAAAYAAAAAH.*"

"What *is* wushu?" Anna asked again.

"You know," Sam said, "kung fu isn't about attacking your enemies; it's about using your enemy's own energy against them."

Sam had his nose in a history book. As usual, he was more than happy to share the information.

Fred was about to attempt a roundhouse kick when his watch began beeping loudly.

"I wish I could figure out how to turn this thing off," Fred said. He tried pushing one button. Then another. And another. Finally, the watch was quiet.

"Would someone *please* tell me what wushu is?" Anna cried.

I would have answered her question . . . if driving her crazy weren't so much fun. Besides I had my own questions.

"Hey, Sam," I said. "Did thirteen monks really take on a whole army? Or did they make that up for the movie?"

Sam flipped through the pages of the history book. "Li Shimin is in here, but it doesn't say anything about the thirteen monks."

"Hey," I said, "I bet it's in *The Book*." I headed toward "the safe" to get it.

Sam looked up, panicked. "Joe," he said. "Don't even think about it. You know what'll happen. We'll warp, get in trouble, and the next thing you know someone will be trying to chop our heads off."

He had a point. *The Book* had gotten us into a few scrapes in the past. I got it as a birthday present from my uncle Joe on my tenth birthday. It's basically a time machine—it can transport us to any place and time in history. While that sounds really cool, there is one problem: Whenever we travel through time, *The Book* has a habit of disappearing. And without it, there is no way to get back home. But I *really* wanted to know about those monks. I opened the safe and gasped.

"What?" Fred and Sam asked at the same time.

"*The Book*—

it's gone!" I cried.

"Wushu," Anna said. "Literally translated, *wu* means 'martial' and *shu* means 'art.' In other words, the study of the art of fighting."

Fred, Sam, and I looked over to see Anna ... reading from *The Book*.

Sam froze.

"Hey," I said. "Where'd you get that?"

"From that cardboard box you keep it in," Anna said.

"The safe!" I cried.

"That's supposed to be a safe?" Anna said.

I was about to throttle her, when Fred interrupted.

"Does it say anything about the monks?" he asked.

Anna flipped the page and pointed. "Oh, look. That thing with the thirteen monks really did happen. They broke Li Shimin out of prison. Wang was—"

"That's *my* book!" I yelled.

"I'm just looking," Anna said.

Clearly her little-sister brain was not grasping what I was saying. Time for action. I tried to yank *The Book* out of her hands.

"Hey!" Anna cried, holding on tightly.

"I don't go digging through your things," I said. "How'd you like it if I raided your diary?"

"That's different," Anna said.

"Hey . . . uh . . . guys," a small voice said. It was Sam. "Guys, don't pull on *The Book*. Don't pull . . ."

But Anna and I were too busy with our tug-of-war to pay much attention.

"Tear that book," Sam said loudly, "and you could rip the entire space-time continuum!"

Just as I gave *The Book* a giant tug, Anna let go. My arm flew back and *The Book* went with it, smashing into Sam. A flash of green light erupted from it, blinding us.

I looked down. My body was still there. Phew. We hadn't warped.

"We're still here," I said. "Sorry, Sam. I think I whacked you pretty hard with *The Book*."

I turned around. "Sam?"

Sam was gone.

"Help! Help!" A muffled sound was coming from *The Book*. I opened it up. There—on the same page as Li Shimin—was Sam.

"What happened? Where am I?" shrunken Sam cried. "Get me out of here." I couldn't believe it—Sam was trapped in *The Book*.

Anna, Fred, and I looked down at *The Book*. We'd had a lot of weird adventures before, but this was a first.

"He must be stuck mid-warp," Anna said.

"Don't worry," I told Sam. "We'll get you out."

Fred poked at the page, trying to help. "Ow, watch it," Sam said.

Green mist started seeping out of *The Book*.

"Stop poking it," Anna said. "You're going to make us warp."

It was too late. In a bright green flash, we all disappeared.

CHAPTER 3

So that's how we got to ancient China. Now Fred was dead, and Anna and I were face-to-face with a crazed madman with some serious wushu.

"'Finished him off,'" Anna said, repeating Angry One's words. She glared at him. "He's just a kid. How could you kill him?"

"I . . . I . . . that's not what I meant," Angry One said.

"Fred never did anything to you," Anna said. "He was just minding his own business when, *bam*, you challenge him to a fight.

You should be ashamed of yourself."

There was no stopping her now. Anna was all fired up, and the angry guy was getting an earful.

"Why don't you pick on someone your own size," Anna said. "You know what you are—"

Fred tapped her shoulder.

"Have you seen my other shoe?" he asked.

"Back there, where he killed you," Anna said, waving her hand behind her.

Still glaring at Angry One, she continued her rant. "You're just a big bully. Fred never . . ."

Then it hit her.

"Fred?!" Anna said.

"Look! He's alive," I said, clapping Fred on the back.

"Ow, ow, ow. Careful," Fred said.

Angry One came over. He looked a little less scary now.

"What I meant to say," he explained, "is that I *could* have killed him. But I am a Shaolin monk, and a monk never kills. He only uses his opponent's energy against him."

"That's what Sam said," I said. "Sam. Where is he?"

"Where's *The Book*?" Anna asked.

Sam was stuck in *The Book*, so wherever *The Book* was, Sam was, too. And right now *The Book* was . . . lost.

The monk turned to Fred. "My apologies," he said. "Please allow me to introduce myself. My name is Tanzong. I thought you were a volunteer for the army I am raising to fight Wang."

"Who's Wang?" Fred asked.

"Wang Shichong is the man who calls himself emperor," Tanzong said. "I call him a bloodthirsty villain."

"Hey, Joe," Fred whispered. "Wasn't Wang the bad guy from the movie?"

Fred was right. This was all starting to sound familiar.

Tanzong continued. "Wang has taken General Li Shimin—the son of the rightful emperor—prisoner. Unless the Shaolin monks find a way to rescue him, Li Shimin will be executed and the country will descend into bloodshed."

"But these are not your concerns," Tanzong said. He picked up the extra fighting staff from the ground.

"May Lord Buddha protect you on your journey," he added. Then Tanzong bowed and walked away.

"Hmm . . . *Li Shimin*," Anna said. "That's what I was reading about when we warped."

"And that's the page Sam was stuck on in *The Book*," I said.

"If we find Li Shimin," Fred said, "we might find . . ."

". . . *The Book*!" Anna said.

We had to get to Li Shimin and to Sam, before someone else did.

"Wait!" we called out, as we raced off after Tanzong.

CHAPTER 4

"Firewood," Tanzong called out as he entered the city center. "Firewood for sale!"

He was dressed like a peasant with a big pointed hat and a fake beard. Fred, Anna, and I were stuffed like sardines into a large basket slung across his back, pretending to be firewood.

See, a good plan always involves two things: (1) a costume and

(2) being really uncomfortable. And Tanzong's plan to sneak us into the city to find Li Shimin and *The Book* was no different.

After he had passed through the city gate, Tanzong ducked out of sight and opened the lid of the basket.

"Here," he said, handing Fred two pieces of flint. "Once you have found Li Shimin, use this flint to set off a smoke signal. We will follow the smoke and free you."

He tipped the basket on its side so we could crawl out. In front of us was a stone building with barred windows. The prison. That's where we'd find Li Shimin and (hopefully) *The Book*.

"Remember," Tanzong said, "a monk does not kill, but Wang does. You must all be very careful." With that, he disappeared.

Fred, Anna, and I quickly shimmied through some open windows, ending up in an empty hallway in the prison.

"Okay," Fred said. "Let's go over the plan.

We sneak around the prison until we find *The Book*—"

"And Sam," Anna said.

"—which is probably with this Li Shimin dude," Fred continued. "We set off the smoke signal. Tanzong flies in and rescues us, *bam*, we warp back, catch the end of the movie, and find out how the big battle of the thirteen monks turns out."

Maybe Fred had seen a few too many action movies.

"Let's synchronize our watches," Fred said.

Okay, he'd *definitely* seen too many action movies.

Fred started playing with his watch, and it began beeping wildly.

"Turn it off!" I hissed.

"I'm trying!" Fred said.

Fred frantically pushed more buttons. Finally, the beeping stopped.

"Whew!" Fred said. "All right, let's—"

But before Fred could finish his sentence, there were some very sharp spears pointing in our direction.

CHAPTER 5

The unfriendly guys with the spears escorted Fred, Anna, and I to our new home—a stone prison cell. Another prisoner sat slumped in the corner, but this wasn't exactly time for polite introductions.

"'Synchronize our watches?'" I asked, glaring at Fred.

"It seemed like a prison-break-y thing to do," Fred explained.

"Maybe if we set off the smoke signal, Tanzong could come and get us," Anna suggested.

"Yeah," I said. "But then we'd just have to break in again. We still haven't found *The Book*, or Sam—or Li Shimin."

The prisoner in the corner turned to look at us. He was a young man in his early twenties. "You are looking for Li Shimin?" he asked.

"Yeah," Fred said. "Do you know him? We're here to bust him out of jail."

"*I* am Li Shimin," the prisoner said, eyeing Fred.

Fred gave the guy a once-over, then leaned toward me. "The guy in the movie was much older," he whispered.

"*You're* the big general they're all talking about?" I asked the prisoner. He didn't look the part.

"*You're* the big rescuers they sent?" He had a point.

But arguing was just wasting time.

We had to break out.

"What about *The Book*?" I asked. "You've got it, right?"

"Book?" Li Shimin said. "I don't have any books. Wang has taken everything from me."

"Maybe it's around here somewhere," Anna said.

We started looking around the cell, but aside from some dirty straw on the floor, it was pretty empty.

"I better start that smoke signal," Fred said, pulling the pieces of flint from his pocket. He walked over to the barred window and began fiddling with the flint.

"I don't get it," I said to Li Shimin. "Why does this guy Wang hate you so much?"

"I refuse to accept him as emperor," Li Shimin explained.

"Why?" I asked. "Is he that awful?"

Li Shimin leaped to his feet. "Wang has killed thousands!" he said. "He stirs up fighting wherever he can and steals land—even from the monasteries. If only I could get out of here, I could raise an army and defeat that tyrant. Then my father would be emperor. And eventually—myself. I have such dreams for China." He looked sadly toward the window.

"Well," Fred said, holding up the flint. "Once I get this baby working, we're home free."

Fred tried to strike the flint dramatically against the stone window frame. But instead, the flint went sailing out the window.

"Oops," Fred said. "Does anybody have any matches?"

"Great," I said. "*Now* how are we going to get out of here?"

"Perhaps I can help?" a voice said.

"Wang!" Li Shimin cried.

"How about some *fresh air*?" Wang said.

Fresh air did sound pretty sweet compared to this nasty prison cell.

Wang gave us an evil smile.

On second thought, the prison cell wasn't *so* bad.

CHAPTER 6

Outside, Fred, Anna, Li Shimin, and I were lined up against a big stone wall with lots of strange little marks in it.

Wang was standing across from us, between two large metal bowls full of burning coals. He motioned with his hand and an archer quickly joined him. Something told me the strange little marks were . . . *gulp* . . . arrow marks.

"Oh, yeah," I said, thinking back to our cozy little prison cell. "This is *much* better."

Li Shimin wasn't helping the situation.

"The throne does not belong to you, Wang. You are a thief," he yelled.

"A thief, eh?" Wang said. "The throne was empty. I took a seat—and a head, or two . . . or four . . . hundred."

"You dog!" Li Shimin cried.

"Yes, I am a dog." Wang said. "And you are a clever fox—even if you did lose . . ." Wang pulled *The Book* from his robes. ". . . your battle plans."

"*The Book*," Anna said.

"Excuse me, Mr. Wang, sir," I said in my most polite voice. "Those aren't battle plans. Just open it and see for yourself."

Wang looked at me suspiciously but opened *The Book*.

As soon as the pages fell open, we heard Sam's voice squeaking out. "At last," he said. "I was afraid I was going to run out of oxygen in here. . . ."

Sam noticed Wang. "Hey," he said. "Who are you?"

"*AAAAAAHHHH!*" Wang screamed.

I guess he'd never seen a talking book before.

"*AAAAAAA AHHHHHHH!*"

Sam screamed back. I guess he'd never seen a giant, screaming evil emperor before.

Wang tossed *The Book* in the air, and it landed on the edge of one of the metal bowls filled with burning coals.

"*AAAAAAAAHHHHH!*" Fred, Anna, and I screamed.

"Sam's going to burn," Anna cried.

"If *The Book* burns," I said, "we'll all go up in smoke."

"That . . . that image," Wang said. "It spoke to me. You are evil sorcerers."

Still shaking, he turned to the archer. "Execute them all. Now," he commanded.

The archer stared down Fred, Anna, Li Shimin, and I.

"I wonder who he'll shoot first?" Fred said.

In one swift motion, the archer plucked four arrows from his quiver and loaded them all in his bow.

"Whoa! This guy's good," Fred said.

The archer took aim.

Fred, Anna, and I gulped. If this were a TV movie, it would have been the perfect time for a commercial break.

CHAPTER 7

"What's all the commotion? I can't see what's going on," Sam called from *The Book*. "Hey— is it getting hot, or is it just me?"

Flames were licking closer and closer to *The Book* . . . and to Sam.

"Fred," I whispered. "If *The Book* goes up in flames, we're all goners. We have to get to Sam."

"Sure," Fred said. "We'll save Sam, right after we're done being killed."

"Archer— prepare to fire!" Wang commanded. "Ready. Aim. . . . Huh?" Before Wang could give the final orders, something distracted him. He saw a figure run across the city wall. Could it be . . . ?

Just then Sam—who suddenly realized what was happening—screamed, *"FIRE!"*

The archer let loose. We closed our eyes.

"AAAAAAAAAAAHHHHHHH!" Fred, Anna, and I screamed. But nothing happened. After a few seconds, we each opened one eye, then the other.

There stood Tanzong—two arrows in each hand.

"Whoa, nice catch," Fred said.

"Don't just stand there," Wang yelled to the archer. "Shoot them!"

As the archer reloaded, Tanzong swooped down and grabbed Li Shimin and Anna. With a swift kung fu leap he jumped to the top of the wall. Fred and I followed.

"Quickly," Tanzong said. "Over the side."

"Wait," Anna said. "We need to get Sam."

The archer was taking aim. This time five arrows were loaded in his bow.

Tanzong thought quickly. He tied a rope around an arrow and hurled it at *The Book*. *THWOK!* A direct hit.

The archer let the arrows fly, just as Tanzong yanked *The Book* and Sam to safety. Once we were over the city wall, Tanzong handed me *The Book*.

A very sweaty and upset-looking Sam glared out from the pages. "That was too close," he cried. "I was baking like a pepperoni pizza. And whose bright idea was it to shoot a giant arrow into *The Book* while I was *in* it! I could have been..."

The best thing about Sam being in *The Book* was that we didn't always have to listen to him. I closed the pages and tucked *The Book* under my arm.

★ ★ ★

We met up with Tanzong's other monk friends in a clearing in the forest. Tanzong and Li Shimin began to scratch out plans on the ground with a stick.

"Wang's supplies come through here," Li Shimin said. "We will block them. If he has no weapons, he cannot fight."

Tanzong nodded.

Fred, Anna, and I sat nearby with *The Book* open so we could talk to Sam.

"So, is Li Shimin going to rule all of China?" I asked Sam.

"Actually," Sam said, "his older brother is in line for the throne first. But from what I've been reading in here, Li beat him to it by . . . getting rid of him." Sam ran a finger across his neck and made a face.

"Whoa! His own brother," I said. Talk about sibling rivalry.

"*But*," Sam continued, "Li Shimin does go

on to unify the country, and China really prospers under him. Arts, education—you name it."

Tanzong walked over. "Thank you again for helping to rescue our general. If there's anything you need—"

"You can show me that arrow-catching stuff," Fred said.

"Such things are not for young children," Tanzong replied. "It takes many years of study to master the art of kung fu."

"Man, I knew you'd say that," Fred said.

"What we really need," Anna said, "is someone to help us get our friend out of this book."

Tanzong thought for a moment. "Hmmm," he said. "That is a very difficult problem. For this you need someone skilled in the magic arts. Someone very wise and powerful."

"Got any ideas?" I asked.

"There is only one man in all of China who can help you," Tanzong said.

Fred, Anna, and I followed Tanzong's eyes as he gazed off to a distant mountain peak.

Something told me this magic man would not be easy to find.

CHAPTER 8

"**A**re we there yet?" Anna said.

"Not yet," I said for the 800th time. We'd been climbing straight up a steep, craggly mountain for over a day. "Why do wise men always live in the middle of nowhere?"

"I just hope this guy will show me some kung fu moves while he's getting Sam out of *The Book. HEE-YAAH!*" Fred said, as he did a spastic kick.

"Hey, Joe," a muffled voice said. "Open up."

It was Sam from inside *The Book*. Reluctantly, I opened it.

"According to *The Book*," Sam said, "we're going to go right by the Great Wall of China."

"No kidding," Fred said. "The Great Wall of China? That thing's like four thousand miles long and one hundred feet high."

"Actually," Sam said. "It's closer to four thousand, five hundred miles. Longer than the distance from New York to California. It began as a lot of little walls around different kingdoms, but kept growing and growing—for more than two thousand years. And did you know that it's considered the Eighth Wonder of the World?"

Sam with his nose in a book was bad enough.

Sam *in* a book was just too much.

"I don't see any Great Wall," I said, looking around. "All that's here is a puny little row of stones. It barely comes up to my knees."

"I guess they're still working on it," Fred said.

We stepped easily over the not-so-great wall of China and kept walking.

Finally, we reached a cave at the very top of the mountain. That's where Tanzong said we'd find Hui-k'o—the magic man.

"According to Tanzong's map, Hui-k'o's house should be right here," Fred said.

"What?" Anna said. "In a cave?"

I peeked into the mouth of the cave. "Hello?" I said.

My voice echoed a few times, but there was no other response.

"Oh great," Sam said. "We came all this way. Over that mountain. Over that "great" wall. For nothing. I'm still stuck in this book, we're still stuck in China—"

"And I still don't know any kung fu," Fred added.

"*Those* are your problems?" a voice said.

We turned and saw a small, old man wearing a worn cloak.

"Bah," he continued. "That's nothing. Try being sixty years old and living alone on a mountain."

"Are you Hui-k'o?" Anna asked.

"I am no one," he responded. "A mere ripple on the river of time."

Fred, Anna, and I sighed.

The man smiled slightly. "But you may call me Master Hui-k'o if it pleases you," he said.

"Can you help us?" I said. "We need you to get our friend out of this book."

Hui-k'o took *The Book* and held it in his hands. It glowed green for a second, and

Hui-k'o nodded wisely.

"Your friend will be released when the time is right," he said.

Hui-k'o handed *The Book* back to me.

"Well?" he said impatiently. "What are you all waiting for? You think the chores will do themselves?"

Hui-k'o looked at me and pointed to a bucket. "You," he said. "Fetch water from the stream. Do not spill a single drop."

Then he looked at Fred and pointed to a shovel. "You. Clean out the stable. And be careful—my horse is very temperamental."

Anna eagerly approached Hui-k'o, ready to receive her orders. "What about me, Master Hui-k'o? What is my assignment?"

Hui-k'o rubbed his chin and thought for a moment.

"You," he said. "Stay out of the way."

"That's it?" Fred said. "You're not going to teach us any kung fu?"

"To the mind that wishes to learn," Hui-k'o said, "everything is a lesson." Then he yawned. "It's time for my nap."

Hui-k'o turned and went into his cave, leaving us to complete the chores.

"He *must* be a wise man," Fred said. "I can't understand a thing he says."

I grabbed the water bucket and handed *The Book* to Anna. "Don't get any ideas," I said. "You're just watching it for me."

"Okay, okay," Anna said. "I'm just watching it."

* * *

For the next few days, we hung around Hui-k'o's and helped around the cave. At least we *tried* to. Who knew fetching water could be so hard? I ended up spilling more than I carried.

the branch. It was heading for the stream.

But before it hit the water, the bucket suddenly stopped in midair. It hovered over the stream and began to glow with a greenish light.

"Huh?" I said.

I whipped around, and there stood Hui-k'o. One hand held his staff; the other was raised in the direction of the bucket. Slowly the bucket began to float toward him.

"Bodhidharma always said the wise man never shows his powers," Hui-k'o said. "But this time, I'll make an exception."

"H-how'd you do that?" I stammered. "Who's Bodhidharma?"

"The father of Zen Buddhism," Hui-k'o said, as he caught the bucket. "And my former teacher."

Fred did his best to shovel out the horse stall. But Hui-k'o's horse had a different idea. I heard a loud *WHUMP*! I turned to see Fred flying through the air. He landed in a heap at the back of the stall. Out cold.

Even Anna had trouble following orders. And all she had to do was stay out of the way.

After three days, we'd just about had it. We were tired and bored, and Hui-k'o wasn't telling us anything. Fred was ready to leave, but something made me think Hui-k'o knew more than he was letting on.

I was taking a catnap down by the stream, when I suddenly heard a voice.

"Wake up!" Hui-k'o yelled. "Dreaming will not fill the bucket."

"I'm awake! I'm awake!" I yelled, hopping to my feet, still half asleep. "Now where did I put that water bucket?"

"Oh, no," I said. There, dangling from a high tree branch, was the water bucket. Just then, a huge gust of wind blew the bucket off

We sat on some nearby rocks, and Hui-k'o explained. "Many years ago he came from India to the Shaolin monastery. The monks were lazy and fell asleep in meditation, so he taught them special exercises. Some say these techniques evolved into kung fu."

"So that thing you just did—with the bucket—that was kung fu?" I asked.

Hui-k'o smiled. "No," he said. "That was something I learned long, long ago . . . from . . . *The Book*."

"So you *do* know about *The Book*," I said.

"I have seen it before," Hui-k'o said. "This book of yours—it is fun. Full of adventures, also. But in the wrong hands, very dangerous."

Hui-k'o gave me a serious look. "The one who had *The Book* before—always, he is looking for it.

Always, he is looking for *you*."

"My uncle Joe?" I said, confused. He's the one who'd given me *The Book*. Hui-k'o didn't answer.

"There is no time to explain," he said. "You and your friends must go back to Tanzong. A great battle is beginning."

"But how can we help?" I said. "You didn't teach us how to fight."

"The danger that awaits you there," he said, "is less than the danger that seeks you here."

I wasn't exactly sure what Hui-k'o meant, but the way he said it sent shivers down my spine.

"Just remember, Joe," Hui-k'o added, "time is in the mind. Control your mind and you can do anything."

"Easy for you to say," I said. "You're a Zen Master."

"Nonsense," Hui-k'o said. "Anyone can control his mind. It's as simple as carrying a bucket of water." Hui-k'o held up the bucket and smiled. But the smile soon disappeared.

"Now go," he said. "Quickly—you are all in great danger."

CHAPTER 9

I found Anna and Fred, and we quickly set off from Hui-k'o's. I had to admit, I was going to miss the weird, old guy.

After hiking down the mountain for hours, Anna, Fred, and I found ourselves in a bamboo forest.

"How are we supposed to find this battle, anyway?" I asked. "Does *The Book* say where it takes place?"

WHOOSH! Out of nowhere, an arrow whizzed past my face, nearly taking off my nose. We were *definitely* on the right track.

Anna, Fred, and I looked off in the distance. We saw what looked like a group of ants moving quickly down a hillside.

"The ground is moving," Anna said.

I took a closer look. "That's not the ground," I said. "That's Wang's army." They were marching toward Li Shimin's troops on the mountain across from them. The battle was about to begin—and Anna, Fred, and I were right in the middle.

The rumbling grew louder as the soldiers got closer.

"This is it," Fred said. "Let's go."

"Wait," Anna cried. "What are we suppose to do? We're just kids."

"Don't you get it," Fred said. "We've been with the wise kung fu dude. We probably know all kinds of kung fu tricks, we just don't know it yet. Let's go!"

"*WASSSSAAAAAAA!*" Fred let out a kung fu battle cry and launched himself into a roundhouse kick. As he came in for a landing, his feet slipped on a pile of wet leaves and shot out from under him. *WHUMP!* Fred landed with a thud. He was out cold once again.

"Leave it to Fred to miss the fight scene," I said.

"Quick," Anna said. "Let's hide him behind that rock."

We dragged Fred out of the way and tried to make a plan.

"What's going on out there? Open *The Book*," Sam said.

Anna opened *The Book*, and set it on the rock to give Sam a view of the action. But the battle was *scary*.

"Uh, okay. I've seen enough," Sam said a millisecond later. "You can close *The Book* now!"

I peered over the rock. The soldiers had almost reached us.

"We need something to defend ourselves," I said. Just then, I saw a staff lying on the ground between us and the soldiers.

"I'm going to try to get that staff," I said.

I raced out into the clearing and bent over to grab the staff.

"Joe! Watch out!" Sam cried. "Behind you!"

I spun around, knocking over one of Wang's goons with the end of the staff. One down, a couple thousand more to go.

"Joe, what do I do?" Anna screamed.

She was under attack.

In a flash, Hui-k'o's words rang in my head.

"Just stay out of the way," I said.

Soldiers charged at Anna full force. As they dove toward her, Anna quickly jumped side-to-side, dodging them left and right. Wang's goons were wearing so much armor, they toppled right over.

"How do you like that wushu?" Anna said.

Anna had finally learned how to stay out of the way. And not a minute too soon.

"Look left, Joe! Left!" Sam shouted from *The Book*.

I spun to my left. The staff swung wildly, taking out two more soldiers. Whatever we were doing—or not doing—seemed to be working. Somehow Anna and I were still alive.

From behind us, a voice bellowed. "Drop your sword, Li Shimin."

It was Wang. He was aiming an arrow straight for Li Shimin, who had arrived with his troops.

"Never," Li Shimin said. "If I must die to save this country—so be it!"

"I see," Wang said. "But are you willing to let an innocent little girl perish as well?"

Suddenly Wang turned the bow and arrow toward Anna. Li Shimin looked at Anna and back at Wang, and then let his sword drop to the ground.

"Ha ha ha," Wang cackled. "I thought you were just weak, Li Shimin. I was wrong. You are gullible as well."

Wang released the arrow. It whizzed through the air—straight for Anna.

"Joe!" Anna screamed.

"Anna!" I screamed.

I had to save my sister. In an instant, everything went blank. I heard Hui-k'o's voice: *Time is in the mind. Control your mind, and you can do anything.*

SLOW . . . , I thought. My mind focused only on the arrow floating through time and space. The arrow glowed a faint green. It slowed down and hovered in front of Anna's face. I reached out my hand and plucked it from the air.

Suddenly everything sped up again.

"How'd you do that?" Anna asked.

"I don't know," I said.

Wang must have been as freaked out as I was. He dropped the bow and scurried off into the forest.

"Quickly, Tanzong," Li Shimin called. "We must catch Wang before he can regroup."

Li Shimin and Tanzong raced off after Wang. There was hope for China after all. Maybe they'd even finish building that wall.

As for us, Anna and I were still alive, Sam was still in *The Book*, and—

"What'd I miss?" a voice said.

It was Fred. He was back in the land of the living. Perfect timing, as usual.

"Oh, nothing," I said. "Just your typical ancient Chinese kung fu battle."

"Man," Fred said. "I was gonna try out my—"

But suddenly we heard a noise. It sounded

like someone clapping. A figure emerged from the forest covered in a cloak.

"Hui-k'o!" I said. Everything suddenly made total sense. I knew I couldn't have stopped the arrow myself—Hui-k'o must have helped me.

"Nice guess, Einstein. But unfortunately—wrong." The figure threw off the cloak and let out an evil laugh.

Anna, Fred, and I gasped. This was *definitely* not Hui-k'o.

CHAPTER 10

Anna, Fred, and I must have been going for a warp record. On this adventure we'd faced certain doom at the hands of a crazed madman not once, not twice, not three times . . . You get the picture. The point is, we were now gazing at another crazed madman who looked equally bloodthirsty and unstable. But, there was something sort of familiar about this one. . . .

"That was an impressive trick, Joseph—slowing down time," the madman said. "My, my, my. You are becoming quite the little warp whiz."

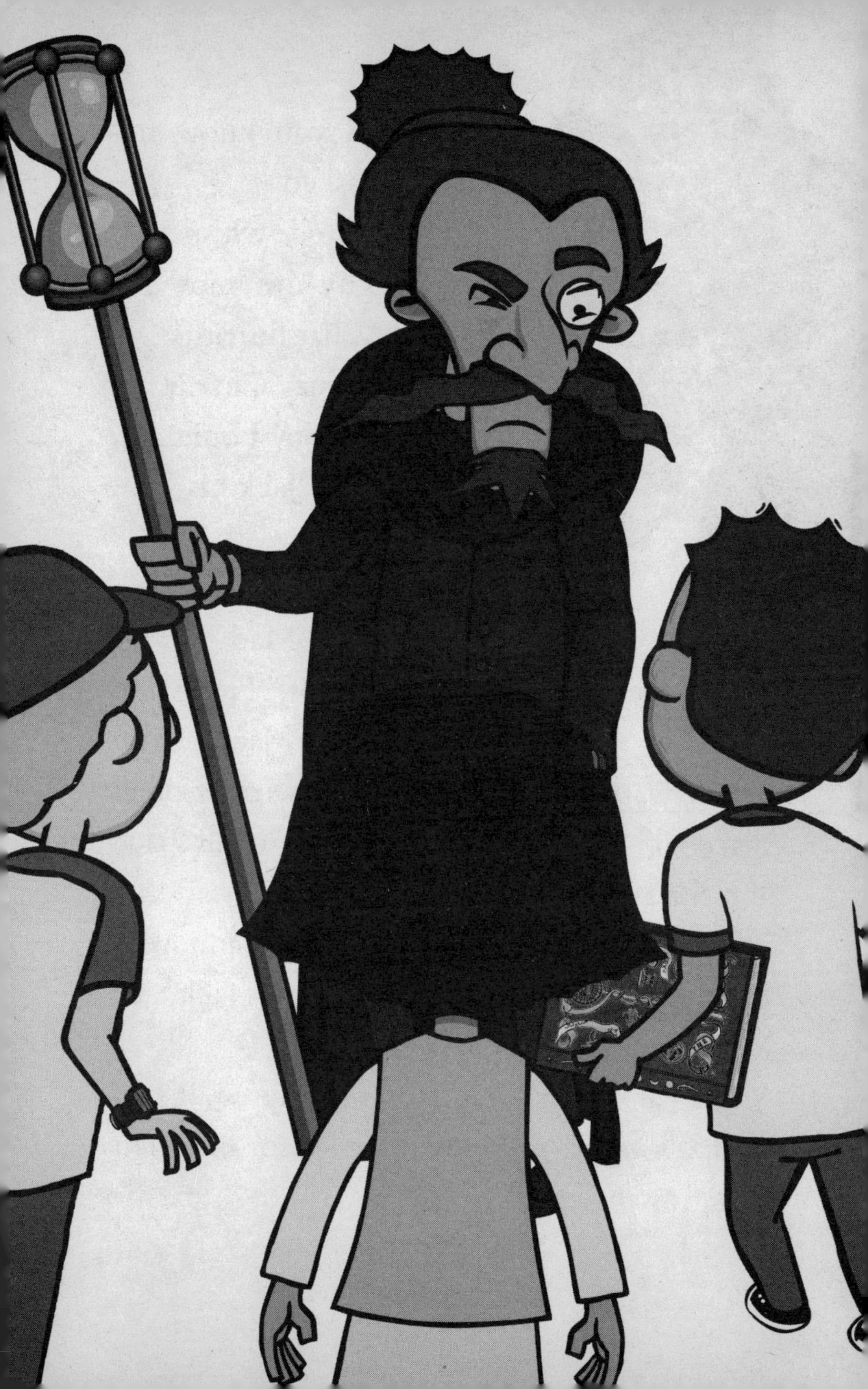

"How'd you know my name?" I asked.

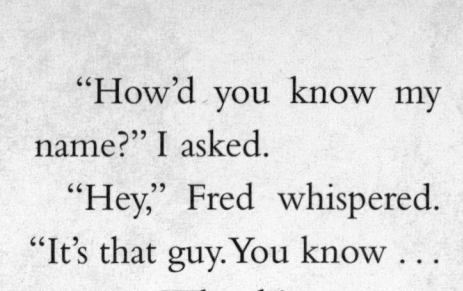

"Hey," Fred whispered. "It's that guy. You know ... Whatshisname ... Crazy Charlie ... Loopy Louie ..."

"Jack is the name," the madman said.

"Mad Jack! That's it," Fred said.

We'd run into Mad Jack before in our warps. He wanted to be the ruler of all space and time. But to be the ruler of all space and time he needed ... *The Book*.

Mad Jack looked at Fred, a little annoyed. "I prefer Stultifyingly Fiendish Jack, or Malevolently Marvelous Jack, or ..."

"What do you want?" I interrupted. It had been a long day, and my patience for madmen was growing thin.

"That's the spirit," Mad Jack said. "Waste no time. Ah, sweet time, my favorite theme. *Time is what I want.* And, lucky me, it's what you have. Hand over *The Book*, dear nephew."

Nephew? Anna and I looked at each other. Were we actually related to this nutcase?

"I knew you looked familiar," Fred said.

"What's happening?" Sam piped in. "I can't see anything in here."

Mad Jack held out his walking stick with a huge hourglass on top, and pointed it directly at *The Book*. Suddenly the stick glowed green and started to buzz. I held *The Book* tighter.

Mad Jack must have known I wouldn't give up easily. He aimed the walking stick at a nearby rock and zapped it into oblivion. Then he pointed the stick at me again.

"How would you like your molecules?" he asked. "Scrambled? Or fried?"

The guy knew how to make a point. I quickly handed over *The Book*.

Mad Jack giggled fiendishly as he stroked the cover.

"What about Sam?" Fred said. "Can you at least let him out of there?"

"And how are we supposed to get home?" Anna added.

"Oh, but you *are* home," Mad Jack said. "Your new home. *Ha ha ha ha!*"

"You don't care about anything but yourself, you big bully," Anna said.

"Au contraire," Mad Jack cackled. "I care *very much* about my precious, precious book!" Mad Jack pulled *The Book* to his face to give it a big fat kiss, but then . . .

WHAM! The cover flew open, nailing him right in the kisser. Mad Jack grabbed his face—dropping *The Book* and his walking stick to the ground.

"For crying out loud," Sam said, "would someone please tell me what's going on out here?"

Sam! We watched as he pulled his top half out of *The Book* like he was coming out of a pool. His bottom half followed. Finally, Sam was free.

"Hey! I'm out," Sam said.

Sam spied Mad Jack and gulped. "Oh, no. I'm out!"

I raced over and grabbed *The Book* before Mad Jack could get his slimy fingers back on it.

I opened it up quickly, and green mist poured out.

Mad Jack scrambled for his walking stick and aimed it in our direction. "Give it back," he hissed. "I command you."

We braced ourselves. There was a blast of green light.

"Nooooooooo!" Mad Jack's scream faded in the background.

We were warping home.

CHAPTER 11

"That was a close one," I said.

We were back in my room in Brooklyn. Anna, Fred, and Sam were sitting in front of the TV, waiting for the movie to come back on. I was putting *The Book* back in the safe, and this time I was using my padlock.

"One second sooner," Fred said, "and we'd be living in a cave for the rest of our lives. No video games. No TV. I owe you one, Sam."

Sam smiled. "Hey, guys, did you hear that? Fred owes me."

I walked over and joined Anna, Sam, and Fred on the floor. "Who knew Mom and Uncle Joe had a brother named Jack?" I said.

"I can see why he's not invited to family reunions," Anna said.

"He must be the one Hui-k'o was trying to warn you about," Sam added.

"I always knew old Hui-k'o knew more than he was telling us," I said.

"What do you think ever happened to Li Shimin?" Anna asked.

"Well," Sam said, "according to what I learned in *The Book*, he went on to become the second emperor of the Tang dynasty. His father was the first. Under Li Shimin, China flourished. The Tang dynasty became a golden age. Culture, education, art, government—"

"Shhhh!" Fred said. "The movie's back on."

This was one kung fu fight scene Fred wasn't going to miss.